The Frog
and
the Footbridge

To: Vincetta, Lisa, Ray, and especially my husband, Mark.

"Oh no," thought Emeril. "I am lost again, and Grandmother will be upset with me for not paying attention to where I was leaping."

Emeril the frog lived with his grandmother in one of the most beautiful locations in France.

His grandmother was always encouraging Emeril to be more observant. "Emeril, frogs have wonderful eyes that help them see all around their heads. You need to use your eyes." Emeril did not pay attention to her.

Emeril was too busy leaping as high as he could. He was an excellent leaper, and his friends would always try to leap higher and farther than Emeril, but they never could. If he would only pay attention when he leaped, he wouldn't get lost so often.

Here he was, far from Grandmother, and the beautiful yellow water lilies where he lived. How would he ever find them again? Off in the distance, Emeril saw a beautiful green footbridge. "If only I could leap on top of the footbridge," thought Emeril, "maybe I could see Grandmother and the yellow water lilies."

Emeril leaped, and

leaped, but the footbridge
was higher than Emeril
had ever leaped before.
He became very tired
from leaping so much.

He finally had to stop to take a rest.

While he was resting, Emeril noticed a reflection in the water. The reflection was of a man sitting on a bench and staring out at the water. "I wonder what he is looking at," thought Emeril.

Suddenly a voice interrupted Emeril's thoughts. "Emeril, I have been looking everywhere for you."

It was Grandmother, and Emeril was so happy to see her.

On the way home, Emeril paid very close attention to the way that Grandmother took him. He used his eyes because he wanted to go back to the footbridge. He was determined to get on top of the footbridge. After all, he was the best leaper around.

derful artist, and he uses his eyes to see the beauty that he will put into his paintings.

"I used my eyes today Grandmother, and I watched very closely, so I can find my way back to the footbridge. Can I go tomorrow? I want to leap on the footbridge and see Monet." At first grandmother said no, but finally she agreed because she thought it would be a good test to see if he had used his eyes.

When Emeril and Grandmother were back home at the yellow water lilies, Emeril told his grandmother all about the footbridge, and the man sitting by the footbridge. Grandmother told Emeril that the man's name was Monet, and he was the person who put the footbridge over the pond. "Why does he sit there and stare," asked Emeril. Grandmother thought for a moment. "Because he is a won-

The next morning Emeril set out to find the footbridge. "Look before you leap," called Grandmother, as he started on his way. Emeril took little hops, so he could stop and use his eyes to check if he was going in the right direction. At last he was right in front of the footbridge. He began to leap as high as he could. He leaped once, twice, three times. "This is not going to work," he thought.

He used his eyes and looked around. Over near the footbridge was a boat. Maybe if I could get on top of the boat, I can leap high enough to reach the footbridge. He leaped on the boat.

Then once again he leaped from the boat with all his might. It worked. He landed right on top of the footbridge. "What a beautiful view," Emeril thought. "I can see why Monet likes it up here. Where was Monet?"

Emeril didn't have to look very far.
Over by the bench, Monet was
painting the most beautiful picture
of the footbridge.

"I can see why Monet looks so
carefully," thought Emeril, "it
helps him to paint such beautiful
pictures."

That night when Emeril came home, his grandmother was so happy to see him and hear of his success. You have finally learned to use your eyes, Emeril," she said.

"Grandmother, if Monet uses his eyes so carefully, why didn't he see me," asked Emeril. "Oh, but Emeril," answered Grandmother…

"I am sure that he did!"